~ FIRST GREEK MYTHS ~
ICARUS, THE BOY WHO COULD FLY

For Alex Speechley
S.P.

WORCESTERSHIRE COUNTY COUNCIL	
374	
Bertrams	01.04.06
JEe	£4.99
RE	

Series reading consultant: Prue Goodwin, a lecturer in Literacy in Education at the University of Reading

ORCHARD BOOKS
96 Leonard Street, London EC2A 4XD
Orchard Books Australia
32/45-51 Huntley Street, Alexandria, NSW 2015
This text was first published in Great Britain
in the form of a gift collection called *First Greek Myths*, in 2003
This edition first published in hardback in Great Britain in 2005
First paperback publication in 2006
Text © Saviour Pirotta 2005
Cover illustrations © Jan Lewis 2003
Inside illustrations © Jan Lewis 2005
The rights of Saviour Pirotta to be identified as the author and
of Jan Lewis to be identified as the illustrator of this work
have been asserted by them in accordance with the
Copyright, Designs and Patents Act, 1988.
A CIP catalogue record for this book is available from the British Library.
ISBN 1 84362 807 4 (hardback)
ISBN 1 84362 785 X (paperback)
1 3 5 7 9 10 8 6 4 2 (hardback)
1 3 5 7 9 10 8 6 4 2 (paperback)
Printed in China
www.wattspublishing.co.uk

~FIRST GREEK MYTHS~
ICARUS, THE BOY WHO COULD FLY

BY SAVIOUR PIROTTA
ILLUSTRATED BY JAN LEWIS

ORCHARD BOOKS

~ CAST LIST ~

DAEDALUS
(Day-de-luss)

A great inventor

ICARUS
(Ik-arr-us)

Daedalus's son

Long ago on the far away
island of Crete, there lived
a boy called Icarus.

His father, Daedalus, was a
great inventor.

He could make all sorts of
clever things, like wooden cows
that mooed and swords that
could fight by themselves.

But Daedalus worked for King
Minos, the evil ruler of Crete.

Icarus and Daedalus lived in great comfort in the king's palace. They had only to snap their fingers and servants would bring them whatever they wanted.

But they could not leave the palace: they were the king's prisoners. There was nothing for Icarus to do and he longed to leave Crete and go out into the world!

One day, Icarus's dream came true.

His father said, "We must leave Crete. The king wants me to build war machines for him now, and I will not do it."

"But how can we get away?"
asked Icarus. "The king keeps a
guard at every door."

"We are going to fly away
from the island," said Daedalus.

Icarus could not believe what he was hearing. He knew his father had made some wonderful things in his time, but could he really make wings that worked?

"What do you think?" asked Daedalus as he opened the door to his workshop. Icarus was amazed.

There were two pairs of giant wings on the table. They looked like real birds' wings but they were made of wax and feathers.

"Beautiful, aren't they?" said Daedalus proudly. "And we are leaving tonight."

"Tonight?" gasped Icarus.

"The sooner we leave, the better," said his father.

That night, Icarus followed his
father up on to the roof of the
palace. Daedalus fastened the
wings to his son's arms.

"I will go first," he said as he
strapped on his own wings. "All
you have to do is flap your arms.
The breeze will carry you along.

"But," he went on, "do not fly too close to the sea, or the spray from the waves will wet the feathers and make your wings too heavy.

"Do not fly too close to the sun either, or the heat will melt the wax and you will fall into the sea."

Icarus was trembling all over.
What if his wings did not work?
What if he fell right into the sea?

Daedalus ran off the roof and stretched out his arms. Suddenly, the wind caught him and lifted him high up in the air.

"Hurry up, son!" he called.

Icarus's legs felt like jelly,
but he took a deep breath and
jumped off the roof.

For a moment, he had the
terrible feeling that he was falling,
then he felt himself soaring.

He opened his eyes and there was the sea far below him, shining in the moonlight. Icarus whooped with joy.

"Look at me!" he called out to his father, and he spun head over heels through the air.

"Be careful!" shouted his father. "We still have a long way to go. Come along."

Icarus sighed. "I am coming!" he shouted back.

But as night turned to day, and the sun blazed high in the sky, Icarus wanted some excitement. "Could he fly higher than the eagles?" he wondered.

Icarus spread his wings and
swooped upwards towards the
sun. Higher and higher he flew,
flapping his wings.

"Whee!" he cried as he flew
faster and faster, and closer and
closer to the sun. Icarus felt like
the king of the world!

Then he noticed a feather floating past his face. Icarus was puzzled – a feather so high in the sky, higher than any bird would ever fly?

He looked at his wings and
suddenly remembered what
his father had said. The sun
was melting the wax.

He had to get away from it,
and quickly!

Icarus flapped his arms as hard as he could, but even more feathers dropped off and floated away.

Wax dripped from the wooden frames and Icarus felt himself falling down, down, down...

...further and further until...
SPLASH!
He hit the water.

By the time Daedalus realised
what had happened, it was too
late. All that was left of Icarus was
a few feathers floating on the sea.

Poor Daedalus was very sad.
He had managed to escape from
King Minos but he had lost his
son doing so. He flew on until he
reached the island of Sicily.

There, he put away his wings and lived alone in sadness for the rest of his life. And all because Icarus had ignored his father's warnings.

⌒ FIRST GREEK MYTHS ⌒

BY SAVIOUR PIROTTA ⌒ ILLUSTRATED BY JAN LEWIS

❏ King Midas's Goldfingers	184362 782 5	£4.99
❏ Arachne, the Spider Woman	1 84362 780 9	£4.99
❏ The Secret of Pandora's Box	1 84362 781 7	£4.99
❏ Perseus and the Monstrous Medusa	1 84362 786 8	£4.99
❏ Icarus, the Boy Who Could Fly	1 84362 785 X	£4.99
❏ Odysseus and the Wooden Horse	1 84362 783 3	£4.99

**And enjoy a little magic with these First Fairy Tales
By Margaret Mayo - illustrated by Philip Norman**

❏ Cinderella	1 84121 150 8	£3.99
❏ Hansel and Gretel	1 84121 148 6	£3.99
❏ Jack and the Beanstalk	1 84121 146 X	£3.99
❏ Sleeping Beauty	1 84121 144 3	£3.99
❏ Rumpelstiltskin	1 84121 152 4	£3.99
❏ Snow White	1 84121 154 0	£3.99
❏ The Frog Prince	1 84362 457 5	£3.99
❏ Puss in Boots	1 84362 454 0	£3.99

First Greek Myths and First Fairy Tales are available from all
good bookshops, or can be ordered direct from the publisher:
Orchard Books, PO BOX 29, Douglas IM99 1BQ
Credit card orders please telephone 01624 836000
or fax 01624 837033
or e-mail: bookshop@enterprise.net for details.

To order please quote title, author and ISBN
and your full name and address.
Cheques and postal orders should be
made payable to 'Bookpost plc'.
Postage and packing is FREE within the UK
(overseas customers should add £1.00 per book).

Prices and availability are subject to change.